The Pooches of Peppermint Park

DOTTIE
and the
DOG SHOW

For my husband, Fred

—T. S.

ISBN 978-0-545-46925-8

Text copyright © 2012 by Teddy Slater.
Illustrations copyright © 2012 by Arthur Howard.

12 11 10 9 8 7 6 5 4 3 2 1   12 13 14 15 16 17/0

Printed in the U.S.A.   40
First printing, September 2012
Book design by Angela Jun and Becky James

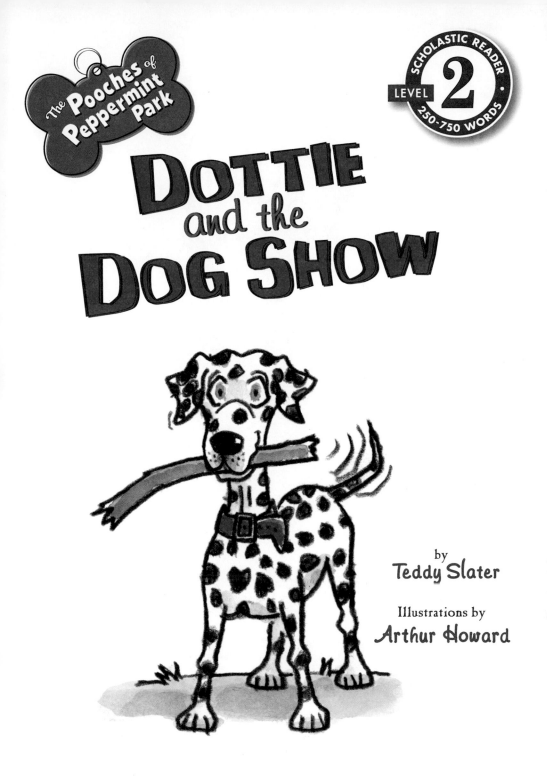

The Pooches of Peppermint Park

DOTTIE and the DOG SHOW

by
Teddy Slater

Illustrations by
Arthur Howard

SCHOLASTIC INC.

Hi!

My name is Samantha,

but you can call me Sam.

Everybody does.

This is my dog.

Her real name is Dorothy,

but I call her Dottie.

Dottie is more than just a dog.

She's my best friend.

We do everything together.

Dottie does lots of doggy things, too.

She sits.

She fetches.

She even rolls over.

My pooch can do all kinds of tricks.

That's why I was so excited about
the Peppermint Park Dog Show.
I just knew Dottie would win a prize.

"Let's sign up now,"
my friend Maggie said.
Maggie and her dog, Skippy, live
next door.

Skippy is a Frisbee champ.
No matter how far or how high
you throw one,
Skippy always catches it.

Bingo and the Baily brothers
live next door on the other side.
Believe it or not,
Bingo knows how to skateboard.

Lulu and Tillie live on the corner.
Lulu loves to sing—
especially when Tillie
plays her violin.

There are lots of other dogs
on our street.

Good dogs!

Smart dogs!

I decided to teach Dottie
a new trick—a really hard one.
"Jumping Through Hoops" looked
perfect.

The book said to start with
the hoop on the ground and to hold
a treat on the other side.
It worked!
Dottie walked right through
the hoop.

The book said to reward your dog
when she does it right.
I gave Dottie the treat
and a high five.
She loves it when I do that.

Next, the book said to hold the hoop

a little higher.

Dottie went through again.

I gave her another treat

and another high five.

I raised the hoop a few inches more.

Now Dottie had to jump for it.

But that didn't stop her.

She took a running start

and sailed right through.

Dottie and I practiced every day
that week.
She never missed. Not once!
There were lots of treats
and lots of high fives.

At last the big day came.

A dog named Barkly went first.

His person's name was Max.

His trick was numbers.

Woof
Woof
Woof

"How much is two plus one?"
Max asked Barkly.

"Woof! Woof! Woof!" went Barkly.

"What's five minus two?"
Max asked.

"WOOF! WOOF!
WOOF!" went
Barkly.
Wow!

Woof
Woof
Woof

After that, Lulu sang,

Bingo rode his skateboard

and a dog I didn't even know
did backflips.

Dottie and I were next.

I could tell Dottie was excited.

She pranced right up on the stage.

I held the hoop the way
I always did.
But this time Dottie didn't
go through it.
She went around it.
Then she raised her paw.

Even though she didn't do the
trick, I gave her a high five.
Then we tried again. And again.
Each time, Dottie went around
the hoop and just did
the high five.

Finally, the judge said,
"Okay. Let's all give Dottie
a hand for trying."
Everyone clapped.

Dottie wagged her tail and
high-fived the judge.

Then it was time for the prizes.
Skippy, Lulu, and Bingo got
beautiful blue ribbons.
So did Barkly.

Dottie kept wagging her tail.

She looked happy and proud.

But I felt like crying.

We had worked so hard

on our trick.

I looked at the judge's table.

There was still one ribbon left.

I knew it couldn't be for us,

but I crossed my fingers anyway.

And guess what?

The judge walked right over to us.

He gave Dottie the ribbon and

a pat on the head.

I gave her a treat
and, of course, a high five.
Good girl, Dottie!